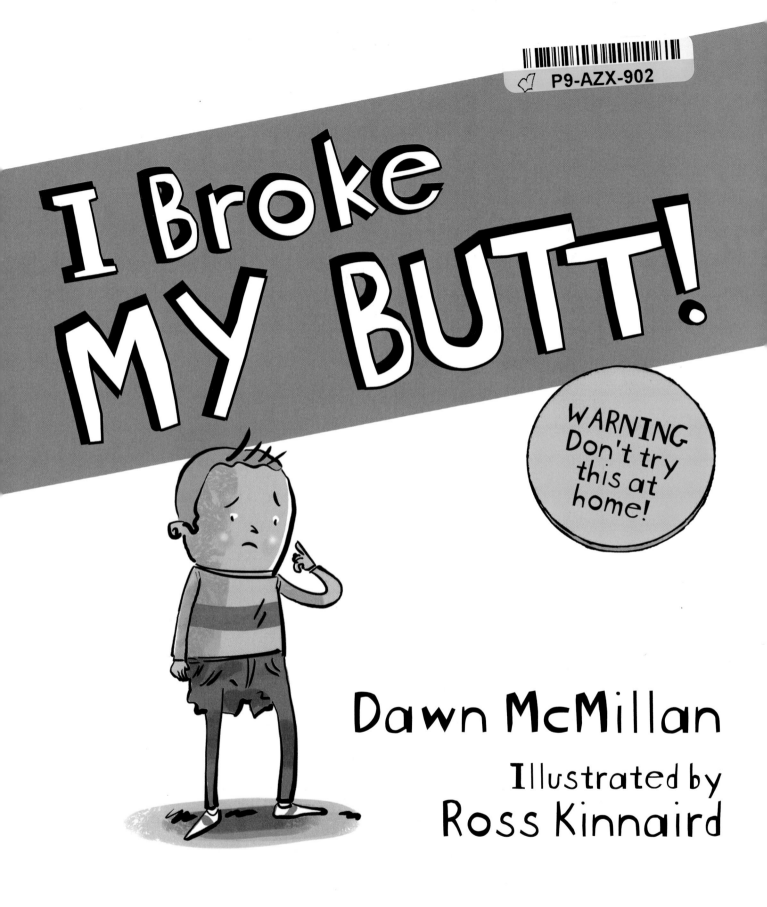

I Broke MY BUTT!

WARNING Don't try this at home!

Dawn McMillan

Illustrated by
Ross Kinnaird

Dover Publications, Inc.
Mineola, New York

I crashed my bike. I sat with a splat!
I broke my butt! My butt has gone flat!

I need to fix it, not a minute to lose.
I head right on home with the broken-butt blues.

Calamity! Catastrophe!

A terrible blow.
My butt bits fall on the floor below.

A disaster, it's true. What can I do?
I have an idea. I'll get some glue.

I see a tray up there on the shelf.
A tray to work on while I fix myself.

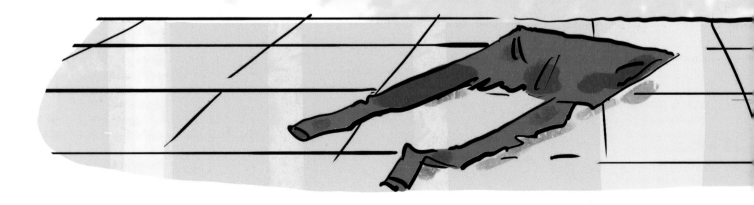

I take all the butt pieces from under the sink.
I glue them together, pink shapes to pink.

Round bits to round bits.
Flat bits to fit.
And ...

Victory! Triumph!

My butt is intact.
I don't mind at all that it still has a crack!

With the pieces together my butt looks like new.
But to put my butt back I'll need GREAT GLOBS of glue!

I'm steady. I'm ready. I press my butt on.
I look in the mirror and ...
Something is wrong!

There's a terrible problem! A problem that's new.
My butt is glued on, but the tray is glued, too.

I twist and I pull. I tug with my might.

I wriggle. I jiggle. But the glue's holding tight.

I think, a butt with a tray is not a good sight.

Am I destined to have a butt with a tray?
How can I dress shaped in this way?

Ah, I have an idea. I see it's quite clear.
I need to snip my pants back here at the rear.

Cut out the back to let the tray through.
A fantastic solution, and easy to do.

But ...

My parents are looking! They may not be kind.
Perhaps they like trays? Maybe they won't mind?

No. My mom wants to fix it, to give it a trim.
Dad has an idea, but don't leave it to him!

Because my new butt is ...

Perfect for sliding in mud or in snow.
I have a built-in sled, ready to go!

Great for sand dunes! I have a blast!
I eat lots of beans to make me go fast!

Perfect for winning
at paintball, you see.

And surfing big waves,
no wipeouts for me!

Hill sliding, too — I didn't see ...

The tree! Crash!

I've broken my butt! What have I done?
The tray has come off. The tray was such fun.

I sit and I think, I wonder and then ...
I go straight back home and I glue it again.

Because...

Being attached to a tray is TOTALLY fine!
See, all my friends want a butt just like mine!

But now ...

I'm going out for dinner.
I need to look like a winner.
I'll dress in my best
with my bright yellow vest.

The dress code? Don't worry, I'll "crack it."
I'll wear my purple and green spotted jacket.

Wait …
This jacket's not right.
This jacket's too tight!
It's not a good fit — a jacket and tray!
What can I do? What can I say?

And then I know exactly what to say …

I say …
Jackets away!

Let's go and play!

About the author

Dawn McMillan lives in Waiomu, a small coastal village on the western side of the Coromandel Peninsula in New Zealand. She lives with her husband, Derek, and their cat, Lola. She writes in her little backyard studio . . . some serious books and lots of silly books, like this one, another butt story!

About the illustrator

Ross Kinnaird is an illustrator and graphic designer. He lives in Auckland, New Zealand. When he's not illustrating a book, or being cross with his computer, he enjoys most activities to do with the sea. He loves visiting schools to draw really funny cartoons of teachers!

Copyright

Text Copyright © 2019 by Dawn McMillan
Illustrations Copyright © 2019 by Ross Kinnaird
All rights reserved.

Bibliographical Note

I Broke My Butt! is a new work, first published by Dover Publications, Inc., in 2019 by arrangement with Oratia Media Ltd., Auckland, New Zealand. The text has been altered slightly for the American audience.

International Standard Book Number

ISBN-13: 978-0-486-84273-8
ISBN-10: 0-486-84273-8

Manufactured in the United States by LSC Communications
84273803
www.doverpublications.com

4 6 8 10 9 7 5 3

2020